W9-AAC-635

SOMEWHERE IN THE WORLD RIGHT NOW

by Stacey Schuett

Dragonfly Books ——✲ New York

To Mavis and Frances,
for seeing beyond the horizon

Copyright © 1995 by Stacey Schuett

All rights reserved. Published in the United States by Dragonfly Books, an imprint of
Random House Children's Books, a division of Random House, Inc., New York.
Originally published in hardcover in the United States by Alfred A. Knopf, an imprint of
Random House Children's Books, a division of Random House, Inc., New York, in 1995.

Dragonfly Books with the colophon is a registered trademark of Random House, Inc.

Maps from *Goode's World Atlas* copyright © 1994 by Rand McNally, R.L. 91-S-244
Used by permission of Rand McNally & Company

Visit us on the Web! www.randomhouse.com/kids

Educators and librarians, for a variety of teaching tools, visit us at
www.randomhouse.com/teachers

Library of Congress Cataloging-in-Publication Data
Schuett, Stacey.
Somewhere in the world right now / written and illustrated by Stacey Schuett.
p. cm.
Summary: Describes what is happening in different places around the world at a particular time.
ISBN 978-0-679-86537-7 (trade) — ISBN 978-0-679-96537-4 (lib. bdg.)
ISBN 978-0-679-88549-8 (pbk.)
[1. Time—Fiction. 2. Geography—Fiction.] I. Title.
PZ7.S3855 So 1995
[E]—dc20
94006223

MANUFACTURED IN CHINA

23 22 21 20 19 18 17

Random House Children's Books supports the First Amendment
and celebrates the right to read.

A Note to the Reader

The earth is constantly turning on its axis. One full rotation takes 24 hours, and during that time, the position of the sun in the sky changes, creating light and dark, day and night.

It used to be that many places measured time from when the sun was highest overhead, at noon. But this meant that neighboring cities would have different clock times at the same instant. Faster travel and better communications made this inconvenient, so in 1884 an international agreement was reached to adopt a system of standard times. The planet was divided into 24 equal areas called time zones. (However, as the maps on the endpapers show, the time zones were adjusted to conform to geographical and political boundaries.) Everywhere within each zone, it is always the same time. When moving from one time zone to the next, there is a change in one hour, forward or backward, depending on whether one is moving east or west.

An important feature of the time zone system is the international date line. As the sun crosses the 24 time zones, somewhere a change in date must occur. The international community needed to agree on a boundary where the new date would begin. It's clear that to have the date change in the middle of a crowded country would cause much confusion, so the line was drawn through the Pacific Ocean, with a few jogs around inhabited regions. Since the earth turns eastward, places west of the date line move into the new date first. So, no matter where in the world you are, there's somewhere else where it's a different day!

*S*omewhere in the world right now, it's deepest night. Fog hugs the shoulders of buildings and bridges. A baker slides long loaves of bread into an oven. Somewhere, somebody watches a movie. A mouse hunts for crumbs.

Somewhere else, in velvety darkness,
elephants sleep standing up, swaying
gently from side to side.

Whales breach and dive in the sea, singing their low, sweet songs. Penguins press close to their chicks to keep them warm.

Somewhere, the night wind sighs and murmurs. The moon shines through a window. A little girl lies dreaming of tomorrow.

But somewhere else, right now, tomorrow is already here. Dawn is breaking. A rooster crows and people are waking up.

Somewhere, it's morning. Families eat breakfast.
Kids get dressed for school. Farmers leave for
the fields to tend their crops.

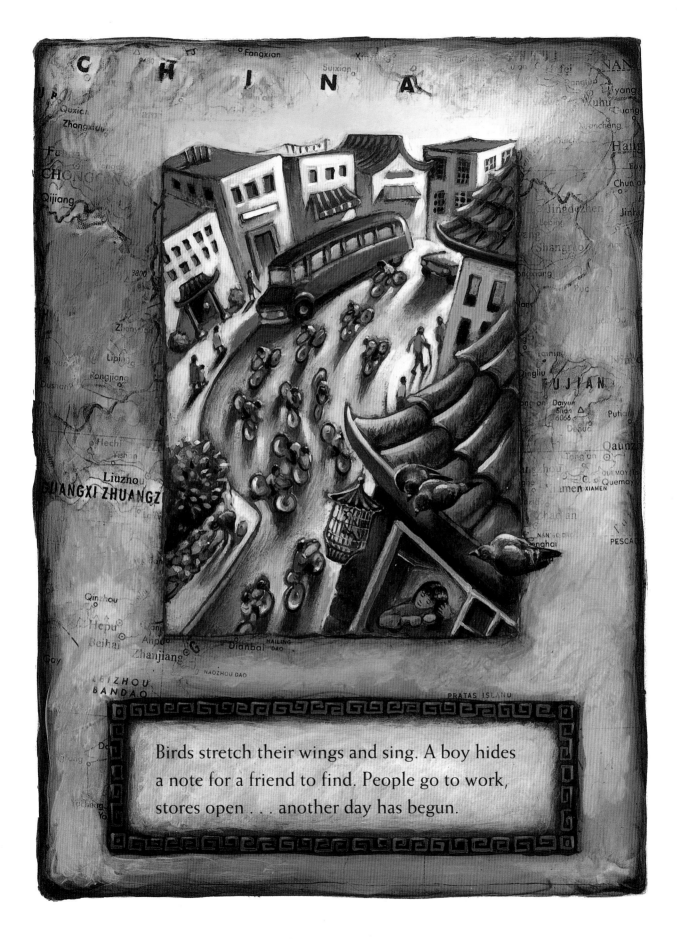

Birds stretch their wings and sing. A boy hides
a note for a friend to find. People go to work,
stores open . . . another day has begun.

And somewhere, right now, people buy food for their midday meal. A carpenter measures wood. A dog runs off with his lunch.

In the late morning shade, a baby kangaroo naps. A koala munches eucalyptus leaves.

Somewhere in the world right now, fishing boats return with their catch. Sea gulls swoop and dive and bicker over scraps.

Somewhere, the afternoon sun gilds workers in the vineyards. Cows graze and rest in the grass. A girl tends her horses.

Somewhere in the world right now, the sun
is setting. Monkeys screech from the trees
as a jaguar glides through the jungle. Parrots
mutter and chuckle. Shadows grow long.

Lake Forest

Highland Park

Winnetka

Wilmette

Evanston

CHICAGO

E.

Chicago

And somewhere else, the sun has already slipped away, drawing evening down like a shade. In the city, signs flash on and off, off and on. Trains whoosh through tunnels, taking people home.

Watseka

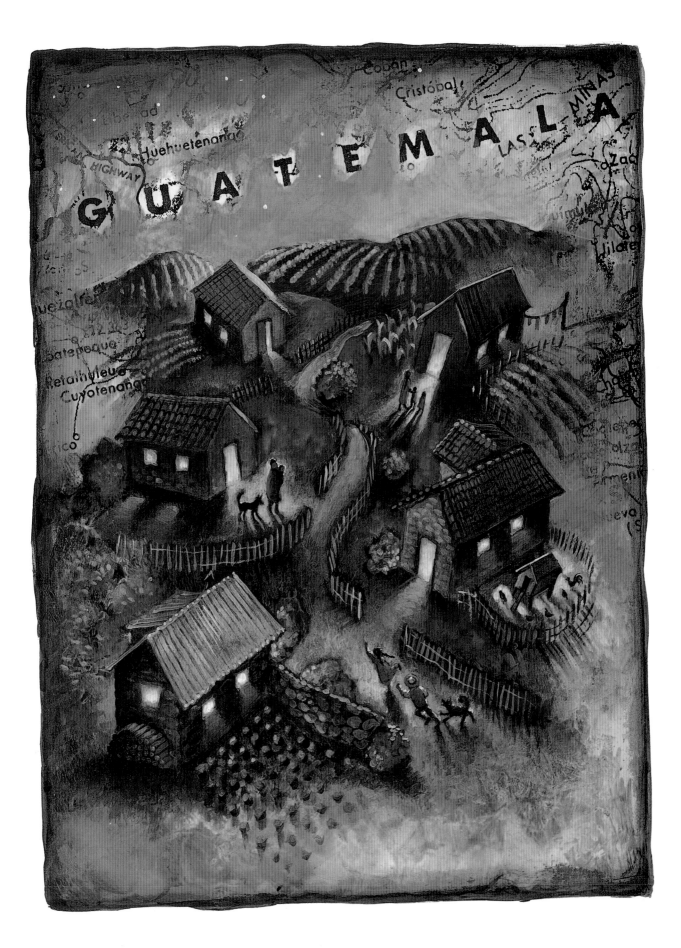

Somewhere, suddenly, houses light up. A girl and her brother race each other to the door.

The day's work is done. A family sits down to supper.

LOUISIANA

Lake
Charles

Biloxi

And somewhere else, night has fallen. Clouds
cushion the moon as it climbs across the sky.
An alligator sleeps in an inky swamp beneath
a tapestry of stars.

The last notes of a song fade into the rhythm of the waves.

Somewhere, a truck driver follows her headlights
down a lonely road. A night watchman starts his shift.

Friends say good night.

Somewhere, somebody reads a story, and someone listens.

Brookline 51

Voices whisper, "Sweet dreams," and under a blanket of night, lights go out one by one, somewhere in the world . . .

right now.